WHO ARE THESE PHUDDS?

They're members of the famous family of de-fective detectives. All over the world, Phudds are on the alert, looking for mysteries to solve—and getting into trouble.

THEY NEED YOUR HELP!

Here's what to do:

1. Start on the first page of each story.
2. Read to the bottom of the page and follow the directions.
3. When you have to make a choice, be care-ful. (The fate of the Phudds is in your hands.)

When you reach an ending, you can start the story over—or begin a new story!

The Orient Express is leaving the station. Turn to page 7 and climb aboard.

DOUBLE-O PHUDD SAVES THE WORLD

Fred Counselor
Illustrated by Marc Nadel

A GOLDEN BOOK • NEW YORK
Western Publishing Company, Inc., Racine, Wisconsin 53404

created by Media Projects Incorporated
and
Mega Books of New York, Inc.

Library of Congress Catalog Card Number: 84-81598

ISBN 0-307-13103-3/ ISBN 0-307-63103-6 (lib. bdg.)

A B C D E F G H I J

Series design by Giorgetta Bell McRee
Ellen Coffey, Project Manager
Bruce Glassman, Project Editor

CONTENTS

The Case of
the Missing Mole

"**I**'m going to the dining car to get us some sandwiches Phustus," Osbert Oswald Phudd, master spy, known as "Double-O," says to his pet mole. They are on a famous train, the Orient Express, speeding through France.

Phustus squeaks his approval.

After walking into a luggage car by mistake, Double-O finds his way to the dining car. He sits down and orders two ham and cheese sandwiches to go. When he gets back to his compartment, he is shocked to find that Phustus is gone!

"Oh, no" cries Double-O. "Phustus has been molenapped!"

Worried and confused, he begins to search the compartment for clues.

"Oh, what has happened to my little buddy!" Double-O says. "I knew I shouldn't have left him alone."

Double-O searches the compartment and comes across two clues.

"Hmmm," he says. "A maid's cap is lying right next to this nice photograph of Phustus." He picks up the photograph.

"Wait just a minute here!" Double-O exclaims. "I didn't take this picture of Phustus! It must be from the molenapper!"

Double-O examines the photograph. A few curly hairs lie on top of it. In the corner of the photograph is a message:

I HAVE YOUR FURRY BUDDY. IF YOU EVER WANT TO SEE HIM AGAIN, LEAVE FIVE THOUSAND FRANCS ON THE CORNER TABLE IN THE DINING CAR.
SIGNED: THE PERSON WHO TOOK YOUR MOLE

GO TO PAGE 8.

Double-O scrambles around the room looking for other clues. He notices a cuff link on the floor.

"Oh, the molenapper must have dropped this," Double-O says. "I have no time to lose. I must go and find my Phustus!"

Double-O stops to think.

"But where?" he wonders. "Should I look for the maid's room or go to the dining car?"

DO YOU THINK DOUBLE-O SHOULD LOOK FOR THE MAID'S ROOM? TURN TO PAGE 10.

SHOULD DOUBLE-O LOOK FOR SUSPICIOUS CHARACTERS IN THE DINING CAR? TURN TO PAGE 13.

Double-O searches for the maid's quarters. He spots a compartment with an open door. A maid without a cap is cleaning the room. Her uniform is covered with animal hairs.

"Did you lose this?" Double-O asks.

"Oh, yes I did, thank you," the maid answers.

"When you were in Room Twenty-seven," says Double-O, "did you see a mole like this one?"

"No," the maid answers. "But I did see the man from Room Thirteen coming out before I went in—a Frenchman, wearing sunglasses just like those. I believe he is in the dining car now."

SHOULD DOUBLE-O CONTINUE ON TO THE MAID'S ROOM? TURN TO PAGE 14.

OR DO YOU THINK DOUBLE-O SHOULD GO TO THE DINING CAR? TURN TO PAGE 17.

from page 13

Double-O is sure. The man and the woman are the guilty ones. He makes his way to where they are sitting.

"Excuse me," Double-O says. "I happened to overhear your conversation about the mole. You may as well give up now. I know you have stolen my little buddy!"

"Well! I've never been so embarrassed in all my life!" the woman says.

"You nincompoop," the man adds. "We were not talking about an animal. We were talking about the mole on Betty's face. And you have some nerve listening in. That was a private conversation!"

The man calls the headwaiter over to the table.

"Waiter, this man has been listening to our conversation." He points to Double-O. "And he is accusing us of ridiculous things. Please remove him from this dining car," the man says.

"Yes, sir, Mr. President," the waiter replies.

"Pr . . . President?" Double-O mumbles.

"Yes," the waiter says. Double-O is dragged out the door. "That was the President of France! You're lucky he did not have you thrown off the train!"

Double-O scratches his head. He sits down, and tries to figure out how he went wrong.

"I know!" Double-O says to himself. "The man with the curly hair! He's the one!"

Double-O gets up and sneaks back into the dining car.

GO TO PAGE 18.

"Excuse me, sir," Double-O asks a man in the corridor. "Have you seen anybody with this mole?"

"No," the man replies. "But I did see a man in the dining car with glasses very much like those."

When Double-O arrives in the dining car, he notices *everyone* in the car is wearing dark sunglasses! Double-O is puzzled. He stands quietly in a corner of the car. He searches for a clue.

One man has curly hair. Double-O becomes suspicious.

"Hmmm, I still cannot be sure he is the molenapper," Double-O thinks to himself. "I need more evidence."

But then Double-O overhears a conversation between a suspicious-looking woman and a man at another table.

"What about the mole?" the man asks.

"I don't like it," the woman answers.

"I like the mole. I think it's nice," the man replies.

Double-O thinks fast. Mole? They must be talking about Phustus! Oh, no, they are the molenappers!

The man with the curly hair gets up to leave. Double-O must make a choice! He can accuse the man and the woman of stealing his pet. Or he can follow the other man.

DO YOU THINK DOUBLE-O SHOULD ACCUSE THE MAN AND THE WOMAN? TURN TO PAGE 11.

SHOULD DOUBLE-O FOLLOW THE MAN WITH THE CURLY HAIR? TURN TO PAGE 20.

Double-O wanders up and down the train corridors. He doesn't trust the maid's story. Why did she have hair on her uniform?

Finally, he finds the door marked MAID'S QUARTERS.

Double-O turns the doorknob slowly. The door is open. He rushes into the room and closes the door behind him.

He hears a growling sound. A ninety-pound German shepherd is facing him!

He reaches for the doorknob and turns it.

"Now I know where the hair on the maid's uniform came from," Double-O says.

Double-O decides to go to the dining car and pick up his investigation from there.

GO TO PAGE 17.

Double-O runs out of the dining car to Room Thirteen.

Double-O tries the doorknob, but the door is locked.

"Drat!" Double-O mutters. "I must use my Special-agent Tieclip Door-opener!"

Double-O begins picking the lock. He hears squeaking inside. He recognizes the voice.

"I'm coming little guy!" Double-O yells.

Double-O feels a hand on his shoulder.

"What do you think you're doing?" a low voice asks.

Double-O turns around. He sees a large policeman.

"Uh...ummm," Double-O says. "I...I'm trying to get my pet mole out of this room here . . . I—"

"Oh, sure," the policeman interrupts him. "And I have a pet dinosaur in my room. Let's go, I am placing you under arrest."

Before Double-O is dragged away, the door opens. Double-O tries to get inside, but the policeman holds him back.

As Double-O is taken away, Phustus pops his head out of the doorway. He sees Double-O being led away by the policeman. Phustus runs down the hall. He squeaks loudly and throws himself down on the floor in front of the policeman.

"So this is the mole?" the policeman asks. Double-O nods. "Oh, forgive me," the policeman says.

Double-O is released. He gives Phustus a big hug.

Phustus squeaks with joy.

THE END

Double-O edges his way a little closer to the man with the curly hair. He notices a camera on his table.

"A camera," Double-O mutters to himself. "It could be the same camera the molenapper took the photograph of Phusty with!"

He continues to observe the man.

A waiter comes over to his table.

"Will there be anything else, sir?" the waiter asks.

"Nothing now," the curly-haired man answers. "I'll have my coffee in my room."

"Which room is that, sir?" the waiter asks.

"Room Thirteen," the man says. "You can bring it there with my check." The man gets up to leave.

Double-O holds his breath. He thinks hard.

"So that's where my little buddy is hidden!" Double-O says quietly.

Now Double-O has to make a decision. Should he go to Room Thirteen to try to rescue Phustus, or should he follow the curly-haired man?

SHOULD DOUBLE-O RUN TO ROOM THIRTEEN AND TRY TO RESCUE PHUSTUS? TURN TO PAGE 15.

DO YOU THINK DOUBLE-O SHOULD FOLLOW THE MAN WITH THE CURLY HAIR? TURN TO PAGE 20.

Double-O arrives in the dining car. There he is met with a surprise. Everyone in the dining car is wearing sunglasses!

"Oh no," Double-O says to himself. "How am I going to find the person who stole Phustus?"

Double-O looks around the room. He stares carefully at everyone in the dining car. Two people catch his eye. They both have sunglasses similar to those Phustus wears. One man sits nervously at his table. He is drinking coffee. He is spilling it on himself and on a camera that sits on his table. Double-O also notices that one of the nervous man's cuffs is open. The other man has blond hair. He is speaking to a waiter. Double-O overhears what he says.

"I will have the french toast please," the man says.

French toast! Double-O thinks. The man must be French!

Which man is the molenapper? Double-O wonders.

DO YOU THINK DOUBLE-O SHOULD ACCUSE NERVOUS MAN OF STEALING HIS PET? TURN TO 19.

SHOULD DOUBLE-O ACCUSE THE MAN WHO OF FRENCH TOAST? TURN TO PAGE 21.

Double-O notices the nervous man's cuff link. It is just like the one he found in his compartment.

"Sir, I know you have stolen my pet mole Phustus. You may as well give up now," says Double-O.

"What are you talking about, sir?" the man asks.

"Why does this cuff link match the one you are wearing?" Double-O holds the cuff link in the air.

"We must both have good taste," the man stutters.

"Your curly hair and your camera helped, too," Double-O announces. "Wait," he says. "I recognize you. You are Carlo Cloo, the most famous detective in Europe."

Double-O calls for a policeman. When the officer arrives, Double-O explains how Carlo Cloo stole Phustus.

The policeman puts handcuffs on the molenapper.

"Drat," Carlo Cloo says. "I wanted to get rid of the mole and ruin that Double-O. I wanted to be the only great detective in Europe!"

"Before you take him away," Double-O asks, "please give me the key to his room. I must go and rescue my Phustus."

The policeman hands Double-O the key and takes the molenapper away. Double-O rushes to the room, and quickly unlocks the door. He gives Phustus a gigantic hug.

"Now we can get back to our vacation," says Double-O. "We really need one after this."

Phustus squeaks a happy yes.

THE END

The man with the curly hair leaves the dining car. Double-O is close behind.

The man walks down the corridor to Room Thirteen. He opens the door and enters.

Before the door closes, Double-O puts his foot in the doorway. The man closes the door on Double-O's foot.

"Ouch!" Double-O cries. "That smarts!"

The man runs inside. Double-O hobbles in after him.

"I know you have Phustus here somewhere," Double-O yells. "I saw the camera on your table. And one of your cuff links is missing. The one you have left matches the one I found in my compartment with the ransom note!"

Double-O sees something sneaking out of a closet—something small and brown and furry. Phustus!

"I must arrest you immediately," Double-O says. Phustus pushes a chair behind the mole-napper and runs out of the way. Double-O advances. The man backs up right into the chair.

Double-O quickly takes out his special Crime-stopper Tying Rope and ties the dazed molenapper to the chair.

"Good work, Phusty!" Double-O says with a smile. "I knew I could count on you.

"It's almost dinnertime, little buddy. Let's go eat," Double-O says. "I would have invited you earlier, little guy"—Double-O laughs—"but I heard you were tied up!"

THE END

Double-O approaches the blond man who ordered french toast. He is determined. He says, "French toast, huh? So you are the man who stole my pet mole Phustus!"

"What on earth are you talking about?" the man says, surprised.

"You ordered french toast. That gave you away, my friend. I happen to know that the man who stole Phustus is a Frenchman!"

"Well, that may be, sir," the man replies. "But I am English. Is there anything wrong with an Englishman ordering french toast for breakfast?"

"Uh . . . well . . . no," Double-O answers in embarrassment. "I suppose not. I'm sorry I bothered you, sir."

"Quite all right, chap," the Englishman says.

Double-O turns around. He looks for the nervous man, but he is gone.

"Now look what's happened," Double-O mutters. "I've lost him. He must have heard me speaking to the Englishman. He could be anywhere by now. Drat. I must go to Room Thirteen to look for the man the maid told me about. I should have gone sooner."

HELP DOUBLE-O LOOK. GO TO PAGE 15.

The Case of the Mona Lisa Mustache

"Look at all these beautiful paintings, Phusty," Double-O Phudd, master spy, says to his pet mole and faithful companion. They are wandering through the Louvre, a museum in Paris, France. Many of the most famous paintings in the world are on display here.

"This red and white one is really exciting," Double-O says. "Look, it says EXIT on it. How modern!"

Phustus squeaks a laugh.

The two friends continue to walk through the crowded museum. A man comes up to them. He looks upset.

"Excuse me, are you the famous Double-O Phudd?" the man asks.

"Why, yes I am," Double-O answers.

"Please come quickly," the man says. "I am Monsieur Lapin. I am the curator of the museum. Something terrible has happened to our greatest painting!"

The curator grabs Double-O by the sleeve. He quickly leads Double-O down the hall into a gallery.

On the gallery wall is the famous painting of the Mona Lisa by Leonardo da Vinci. It is surrounded by many confused tourists. But something is wrong.

"Look at this! Someone has painted a mustache and glasses on the famous Mona Lisa!" the curator shouts.

"You mean the woman in the painting is not supposed to have a mustache and glasses?" Double-O asks.

GO TO PAGE 25.

"No! This is the most terrible thing I have ever seen!" the curator says.

Double-O begins looking around the painting.

A small piece of red cloth is hanging from the left-hand corner of the frame.

"Hmmm, somebody ripped his red shirt on the corner of the frame," Double-O says.

Double-O continues his search. As he gazes at the floor, he sees three things: a puddle of black paint, an artist's paintbrush, and some crumpled candy wrappers. The wrappers trail into the next gallery.

"Well, I can see I have a few clues. I can start my investigation," Double-O announces. "But which ones should I find out about first? The mysterious painter must have been eating candy. And the painter's jacket must have been ripped by the frame."

SHOULD DOUBLE-O SEARCH THE MUSEUM FOR SOMEONE WITH A TORN RED SHIRT?
TURN TO PAGE 26.

SHOULD DOUBLE-O FOLLOW THE TRAIL OF CANDY WRAPPERS?
TURN TO PAGE 33.

"I think this piece of torn clothing is the best clue," Double-O tells Phustus.

Phustus points his paw at the floor.

Double-O looks down.

"Hmmm," he says. "Footprints. Black footprints. They lead back in the direction we came from. It looks like they were made with black paint. Just like the paint on the Mona Lisa."

Phustus continues to squeak.

"Yes, Phusty, I know. We should follow the footprints," Double-O says. "But what about that odd-looking painter over there at the easel?

IF YOU THINK DOUBLE-O SHOULD QUESTION THE PAINTER, TURN TO PAGE 30.

IF YOU THINK DOUBLE-O SHOULD FOLLOW THE FOOTPRINTS, TURN TO PAGE 35.

Double-O and Phustus walk over to the painters. They want to take a look at what the painters are doing.

The man with the mustache and glasses is painting a colorful bowl of flowers. The man with the torn jacket is standing in front of a big blank sheet of paper on an easel.

Double-O speaks to the man with the torn jacket.

"Excuse me, sir," Double-O says. "I am looking for a suspicious painter. Someone has painted a mustache and glasses on the Mona Lisa."

"Yes, someone just told me about that," the man answers. "But I don't know anything. I've been busy painting for the last three hours."

"I see," Double-O says. Phustus lets out a squeak.

"But I think I know the man you should arrest," the painter says in a low voice. "That man over there. He has the same mustache and the same glasses as on the Mona Lisa!"

Double-O stops to think. Phustus begins tugging on his pants leg.

"I know, Phusty," Double-O says. "We are awfully close to the man who ruined the Mona Lisa. But whom should I accuse?"

IF YOU THINK DOUBLE-O SHOULD ACCUSE THE MAN WITH THE MUSTACHE AND GLASSES, TURN TO PAGE 31.

IF YOU THINK DOUBLE-O SHOULD ACCUSE THE MAN WITH THE BLANK SHEET OF PAPER, TURN TO PAGE 36.

CHOC-O CHOC-O

Phustus begins to jump up and down, squeaking loudly.

"Let's follow the trail of candy wrappers, little buddy," Double-O says. "I think they might take us to the person we are looking for."

"Aha!" Double-O announces at the end of the next gallery. "The end of the trail."

Standing at the end of the trail is a little boy, holding his mother's hand. He is eating candy and dropping the wrappers on the floor.

"Excuse me, madam," Double-O says. "I believe you have a little painter on your hands. Your son has painted a mustache on the Mona Lisa!"

"How dare you say that!" the mother cries.

"We have found a trail of his candy wrappers. It leads from the painting to where you now stand," Double-O says. "Your son must be the painter."

"I told you not to throw those wrappers on the floor, Reginald," the mother says to her son.

"I have been with my son every minute. He could not have done such a thing," the mother explains. "Besides, he has no paintbrush and no paint!"

Double-O reaches down to pat the boy on the head.

The boy bites Double-O's hand.

"I think we must be leaving," says Double-O to Phusty. "We have to go back and question the two painters."

GO TO PAGE 27.

Double-O approaches the odd-looking painter.

'Somebody has painted a mustache and glasses on the Mona Lisa," Double-O says. "Have you seen anyone who might have done that?"

"No, I haven't," the painter answers. "I just arrived. I haven't even begun to paint yet. But I did hear someone talking. She said she saw a man with a paintbrush running away from the Mona Lisa and into office Number Twelve."

Should Double-O believe what the painter said, and go to office Number Twelve? Or should he ask the painter a few more questions?

TO GO TO OFFICE NUMBER TWELVE TO FIND THE CRIMINAL, TURN TO PAGE 37.

TO CONTINUE TO QUESTION THE PAINTER, TURN TO PAGE 34.

Double-O walks over to the man with the mustache and glasses. He points his finger at him.

"You sir, are the man. You painted the mustache and glasses on the Mona Lisa!" Double-O announces.

Phustus hides behind Double-O.

"How dare you, sir," the man cries.

"You have the same glasses and the same mustache. It must be you!" Double-O says.

"Let me tell you something, smart aleck. I happen to be the man who gave the museum one million francs last year! I am the rich and famous Count of Monterey! And I do not like your saying that I look like the Mona Lisa!"

"Uh . . . well . . . I'm terribly sorry, sir. I—" Double-O mumbles.

"Now go away. Leave me alone, or I will call the guard! I can have him put you under arrest!" the man says.

Double-O turns to Phustus. He says, "Just a minor mistake on our part, little buddy."

Phustus nods.

"We'd better go talk to the painter with the torn jacket again," says Double-O.

GO TO PAGE 36.

Double-O decides to follow the trail of candy wrappers. He and Phustus make their way into the next gallery. Phustus squeaks and tugs on Double-O's pants leg.

"What is it, Phusty?" Double-O asks.

Phustus is pointing to two painters.

Double-O notices that one painter has a mustache and glasses—just like the ones painted on the Mona Lisa. Then he notices something else. The other painter is wearing a red jacket. The jacket has a tear in the right sleeve.

"I see what you mean, Phusty," Double-O says quietly. "But what about this trail of candy wrappers? It doesn't end here. It leads out to the next gallery."

Phustus squeaks louder.

"Yes, yes, I know. But we must decide what to do now."

IF YOU THINK DOUBLE-O SHOULD WALK OVER AND QUESTION THE TWO PAINTERS, TURN TO PAGE 27.

IF YOU THINK DOUBLE-O SHOULD CONTINUE TO FOLLOW THE TRAIL OF CANDY WRAPPERS, TURN TO PAGE 29.

Double-O walks back over to the painter.

"I'm sorry to bother you," Double-O says. "But did you say that you just arrived? Did you say you haven't begun to paint anything yet?"

"Yes," the painter replies. "That is exactly what I said."

Double-O looks down at the painter's shoes. On the tips of both are spots of black paint. And the spots look fresh.

"If you have just arrived, why are there spots of fresh black paint on your shoes?" Double-O asks.

"And why do those candy wrappers on the floor match the wrappers I found near the Mona Lisa!" Double-O says.

"Phusty, go and get the museum guards. We must have this man taken away!" Double-O tells his pet.

Phustus returns with the guards. The painter is handcuffed and taken away.

"You would never have caught me if you didn't have a good detective on the case!" the painter says as he is taken out of the room. "I was only trying to get some of my work hung in the museum!"

Double-O and Phustus turn and look at each other. They both have great big smiles on their faces. They shake hands. Double-O says, "Another job well done, little buddy!"

Phustus squeaks in agreement.

THE END.

"Okay, Phusty," Double-O says. "We'll do it your way."

Double-O takes out his magnifying glass. He begins to track the mysterious footprints.

"This is very interesting," Double-O says to his pet. "These footprints seem to lead us back where we came from. The criminal must have been following us! How clever!"

Double-O can see where the footprints are going. They lead to the gallery where the Mona Lisa is.

"Well!" Double-O says. "Now we are getting somewhere! These footprints take us right to the scene of the crime!"

There is a large puddle of black paint in front of the Mona Lisa.

Phustus starts to giggle.

"What's so funny, little guy?" Double-O asks.

Phustus points to Double-O's shoes.

Double-O bends over. He looks at the soles of his shoes.

"Oh no," Double-O says, laughing. "These footprints are mine! I must have stepped in the puddle of paint."

Phustus laughs louder.

"But wait," Double-O says. He stops laughing. "We'd better hurry back to the room where that painter was. I think he was the man we are looking for!"

Double-O and Phustus run back to the room where they saw the odd-looking painter.

GO TO PAGE 30.

Double-O and Phustus walk back to speak to the painter with the torn jacket.

"The man with the mustache is not the man we are looking for," Double-O says with pride.

"What are you talking about?" the painter asks.

"You said you have been painting here for the last three hours," Double-O says. "Then tell me why don't you have a paintbrush? And why haven't you painted anything?"

"Drat!" the painter says.

"You cannot fool the great Double-O Phudd! You are the man who almost ruined the famous Mona Lisa!" Double-O announces.

"I had to do it. I am a great painter. But this museum has not displayed any of my work!" the painter says.

"That is no excuse," Double-O answers.

Double-O calls the guard, who is standing outside the gallery.

"Guard, arrest this man," orders Double-O. "He has painted a mustache on the Mona Lisa."

"Yes, sir," answers the guard.

The painter is taken away. Double-O reaches down to shake the paw of his little furry buddy.

"Good job Phusty," Double-O says. "We've done it again!"

THE END

Double-O arrives at office Number Twelve. He places his hand on the knob, opens the door, and runs inside. A man is sitting at a desk, talking on the phone.

"Now I have you," Double-O announces. "You might as well get off the phone and come with me."

"What on earth are you talking about?" asks Rene Lapin, the curator of the museum.

"I . . . I . . . thought you were the criminal— the one who painted the mustache and glasses on the Mona Lisa," Double-O stutters. "I'm sorry to have bothered you. A man in the other room told me the criminal was in here."

"Since when do you listen to the stories of strangers?" the curator answers. "That was probably the man who really did it! Now why don't you go back out there and try to find him?"

Double-O and Phustus inch quietly out of the curator's office and go back to the room where they saw the painter.

When they arrive the room is empty—except for a pile of candy wrappers on the floor where the mysterious painter was standing.

"Nothing but a pile of candy wrappers here, Phusty," Double-O says. "It's a good thing we're on vacation. It looks like we really need one."

Phustus squeals in agreement.

THE END

The Case of
the Melting Mountains

The Orient Express train grinds slowly to a stop. Double-O Phudd, master spy, looks out the window at the Alps of Switzerland.

"Look at those snowy mountains," Double-O says to Phustus, his pet mole. "Aren't they the prettiest things you've ever seen?"

Phustus squeaks a yes.

Double-O and Phustus get their luggage off the train. They walk briskly toward a ski lodge.

"It's been a while since we've been skiing, little buddy," Double-O says. "I hope I remember how!"

Double-O and Phustus check in at the lodge. Then they head for the ski lift.

Double-O and Phustus put on their skis.

The ski lift takes them up, up, up. Soon they reach the top. They are on one of the biggest mountains in the Alps. Double-O turns to Phustus.

"All ready, little guy?" Double-O asks, smiling.

Phustus squats down in racing position.

"Okay," Double-O says. "One, two, three . . . go!"

Double-O and Phustus push off and whiz down the mountain.

Suddenly, Double-O and Phustus go flying through the air. They land on a patch of grass. The snow on the trail has melted.

"Are you okay, little buddy?" Double-O asks.

Phustus shakes the snow off his head. He squeaks a yes.

"Look down there," Double-O says, pointing. "All the snow has melted. The ski trail is bare. How could that have happened?"

GO TO PAGE 41.

Phustus turns around. They have landed in front of a fork in the trail. Two signs point in opposite directions. Phustus stabs his paw at the signs.

"Yes," Double-O answers. "I see. One sign says TO THE BLIZZARD TRAIL. The other says—oh, no—TO Z. PHUDD LABORATORIES."

Phustus starts to jump up and down. He is nervous.

"So that's who's behind all this," Double-O says. "My evil cousin Zoltan Phudd. Let's follow one of these two signs. I'll bet we can track him down. Look at the Blizzard Trail. There is no snow on it either. Should we take a walk down that way? Or should we visit the laboratory? Maybe Zoltan is working there. I just don't know."

SHOULD DOUBLE-O CHECK OUT THE BLIZZARD TRAIL? TURN TO PAGE 42.

SHOULD DOUBLE-O FOLLOW THE SIGN TO ZOLTAN PHUDD'S LABORATORY? TURN TO PAGE 45.

Double-O and Phustus walk down the Blizzard Trail for a while. They come to a fork in the trail. Looking to the left, they see a line of electrical poles strung with high wires. To the right Double-O sees a giant mound of snow.

"Hmmm," Double-O says. "We may have found all the snow, Phusty. But those electrical poles could be a clue also.

"We can follow those poles down the trail to our left. Or we can look for clues around that giant mound of snow."

SHOULD DOUBLE-O FOLLOW THE ELECTRICAL POLES? TURN TO PAGE 46.

OR DO YOU THINK DOUBLE-O SHOULD TAKE A CLOSER LOOK AT THE GIANT MOUND OF SNOW? TURN TO PAGE 53.

from page 45

"We have to jump in through this window," Double-O says. "We must stop Zoltan. He wants to flood Europe!"

Double-O ties his special Swiss Alps Swinging Rope to a post on the roof. Then he and Phustus swing in through the window—a little too far. He and Phustus land in a giant fishnet.

"Aha!" Zoltan cries. "It's my good cousin Osbert. That net should hold you for a while. Soon I will put my last giant hair dryer in place. Then I will turn them all on!"

Zoltan wheels a giant hair dryer out the door. He has escaped. And Europe is in danger! Double-O and Phustus scramble in the net, trying to get free.

Thinking fast, Phustus chews a hole big enough for him and Double-O to crawl through.

When they are free, Double-O and Phustus run outside. They soon spy snowmobile tracks leading over a hill to the right.

Double-O and Phustus jump into a nearby snowmaker. Phustus drives as Double-O keeps an eye out for tracks. At the foot of the northern mountain there are two sets of tracks in the snow. Snowmobile tracks lead off over a hill to the left. Snowshoe tracks lead up the mountain to the right. And there are two thin tracks beside them.

SHOULD DOUBLE-O FOLLOW THE SNOWMOBILE TRACKS? TURN TO PAGE 47.

OR DO YOU THINK DOUBLE-O SHOULD FOLLOW THE SNOWSHOE FOOTPRINTS? TURN TO PAGE 51.

"Let's take a look at old Zoltan's laboratory," Double-O says to his furry friend.

Double-O and Phustus walk. They see a large building in the distance. Smoke is coming out of the chimney. Some snow-making machines and snowmobiles are parked nearby.

"Jumpin' jiminy," Double-O yells. "Look at that!"

Double-O points to each mountain around the laboratory. On the tops stand giant hair dryers.

"Those must be Zoltan's! He's melting the mountains!" Double-O says. "We must stop him."

Double-O and Phustus go down to the laboratory. They see wires leading into a small building. Signs on the building warn, HIGH VOLTAGE. KEEP OUT.

"This must be where the dryers are plugged in," Double-O tells Phustus.

Under a large window they spot a ladder on the ground. He and Phustus climb up and look inside. They see Zoltan, working on one of his giant hair dryers.

"Soon I will melt the Swiss Alps. Heh! Heh! Heh!" Zoltan laughs. "Europe will be flooded! I will buy all the land cheap and turn off the dryers. I will be rich!"

"What should we do?" Double-O asks Phustus.

DO YOU THINK DOUBLE-O SHOULD JUMP INTO THE LABORATORY TO STOP ZOLTAN? TURN TO PAGE 43.

SHOULD DOUBLE-O TRY TO UNPLUG THE HAIR DRYERS? TURN TO PAGE 49.

Double-O and Phustus follow the poles. They come to a clearing. They see a large building.

"This must be Zoltan's laboratory," Double-O says.

Phustus looks around. He begins jumping up and down. He points to the electric poles.

"I see," Double-O says to his excited friend. "The poles lead over that frozen pond."

On the other side of the pond is a shed. The sign says ELECTRICITY. Double-O spots the shed.

Phustus points across the pond.

"Should we go to the shed?" Double-O asks.

DO YOU THINK DOUBLE-O SHOULD CROSS THE POND TO THE ELECTRICITY SHED? TURN TO PAGE 50.

SHOULD DOUBLE-O LOOK INSIDE THE LABORATORY? IF YOU THINK SO, TURN TO PAGE 52.

"We'd better follow the snowmobile tracks," Double-O says. "He must have driven off that way, Phusty."

Phustus swings the snowmaker to the left. Then he speeds up over the hill.

The snowmaker zooms over the hill. Double-O and Phustus are suddenly flying high in the air. They have driven off a cliff!

Double-O and Phustus jump out of the snow-maker. They grab a large icicle hanging from the cliff.

Double-O looks down. He can see Zoltan at the bottom of the mountain. Zoltan is wheeling one of his giant hair dryers to the foot of the hill.

"There he is!" Double-O cries. His voice echoes down the mountains. And the icicle begins to crack.

"Oh, no, Phusty!" cries Double-O.

The icicle cracks in half. Double-O and Phustus tumble down the mountain. Soon they are rolling down the hill in a giant snowball.

They roll and roll. All of a sudden, they stop. When they peek their heads out, they cannot see Zoltan anywhere. A head pops out from under the giant snowball.

"Darn it all!" Zoltan says. "You crushed my plans! My giant dryer is ruined."

"Well, of course," says Double-O. "That will teach you to fool with the great Double-O Phudd!"

Phustus giggles.

THE END

MAIN
SWITCH

Double-O and Phustus quickly climb down the ladder. They run into the building marked HIGH VOLTAGE, KEEP OUT.

Double-O opens the door and goes in. Phustus follows.

"It's awfully dark in here," Double-O says.

Double-O and Phustus walk carefully through the darkness. They can barely make out a shape in the middle of the floor. It is a large box with a sign on it.

Double-O lights a match. He reads the sign.

"It says MAIN SWITCH," Double-O announces. Many wires lead to the box. "We can stop Zoltan if we turn this off."

Double-O opens the lid on the box. He looks inside.

"I think this red switch is the one we want," Double-O says. He reaches inside and flicks the switch.

A burst of light fills the room.

Zap! goes the box. Double-O and Phustus get electric shocks.

"Ouch!" Double-O yells. "That smarts!"

When the light goes off, Double-O and Phustus are standing in the dark. Double-O strikes a match.

"We should have tried to stop Zoltan when we had the chance," Double-O says to his friend.

Phustus's ski cap is still smoking.

"I've got an idea," Double-O suggests. "I think we should try water-skiing next."

Phustus squeaks a smoky yes.

THE END

"Very well," Double-O says to Phustus. "We will cross the pond. And we will try to turn off the electricity."

Double-O and Phustus begin to walk across the ice-covered pond.

They hear a cracking sound.

"Did you hear something, Phusty?" Double-O asks.

Phustus shakes his head.

They keep walking. They hear the cracking sound again. This time it is louder. They stop.

"Oh, no!" Double-O yells. He grabs Phustus in his arms. "The ice is cracking! If we hurry we can make it to the other side."

The ice breaks up just as Double-O and Phustus safely cross the pond.

"Phew! We just made it!" Double-O says. "Let's go look inside the electricity shed."

When they get there, Double-O tries to turn the doorknob.

"Drat!" Double-O says. "It's locked! Now what do we do? We have no way to get back across the pond! We are trapped here until the ice freezes again. That could be days!"

Phustus points toward a bridge down the road.

"Good work, Phusty!" says Double-O.

Double-O and Phustus cross the bridge. They decide to return to the laboratory. They have to see what is inside.

GO TO PAGE 52.

"Those snowshoe footprints look odd, Phusty," Double-O says to his friend. "And those other tracks look like they were made by wheels. The wheels on the giant hair dryer! Let's go!"

Phustus drives the snowmaker up the mountain.

They soon reach the top. Zoltan is standing his giant hair dryer up in the snow. He is getting ready to turn it on.

"Hold it right there!" Double-O yells. "We've got you!"

"Nothing can stop me now!" Zoltan yells back. "My job is almost complete! Heh! Heh! Heh!"

"Not so fast, Zoltan," Double-O answers. "Phusty, let him have it."

Phustus giggles. He turns the snowmaker on and points it at Zoltan.

Zoltan and the hair dryer are quickly buried under a heap of snow. Zoltan pushes his head out at the top.

"Blast it all!" Zoltan yells.

"That should keep you cool for a while," Double-O says. "At least until the police come and pick you up."

Double-O pats Phustus on the back. Then the two heroes drive toward the ski lodge. They will tell everyone their story. They have saved Europe. And they have stopped the mean and nasty Zoltan once and for all. For now.

THE END

Double-O finds a ladder in the snow near the laboratory. He rests it against the building. He and Phustus climb up to the window and stare inside.

"There is Zoltan," Double-O whispers to Phustus. "He is working on a giant hair dryer. He probably used that on the trails—to melt the snow.

"We must take him by surprise, Phusty," Double-O says. "Let's jump through this window on my Swiss Alps swinging rope. Then you can quickly pull out the electric cord on the hair dryer. I will arrest nasty old Zoltan."

Phustus jumps up and down with excitement.

Double-O swings in through the window. He lands on the floor in front of Zoltan.

"We've got you now, Zoltan," Double-O yells.

Phustus quickly runs to the dryer. He pulls out the electrical cord.

"Curses!" Zoltan yells. "I was so close to finishing my project! I wanted to melt the Swiss Alps. Everyone would know about the great Zoltan Phudd at last!"

"Too bad, Zoltan," Double-O answers. "You cannot succeed in your evil plans. The great Double-O Phudd is on the job."

Phustus squeaks loudly.

"Oh, yes, I almost forgot," Double-O adds. "And the great Phustus, too!"

THE END.

Double-O and Phustus approach the mound of snow. They circle around it and find an opening.

"Looks like a snow cave," Double-O says. "I wonder what's inside."

Phustus grabs hold of Double-O's ski pants. He pulls Double-O toward the opening.

"Okay, little buddy," Double-O says. "We'll go inside and see."

Inside, it is dark and cold. Large tunnels branch off in many directions.

"Doesn't look like there's anything in here," Double-O says, looking at Phustus. Phustus begins to tremble.

"What is it, little buddy?" Double-O asks.

Phustus points over Double-O's shoulder.

Double-O turns around. Up on its hind legs, a big brown bear is standing behind him. The bear growls. It begins to move toward Double-O.

"Come on, Phusty," Double-O says. "I think we'd better get out of here. And fast!"

Phustus jumps up onto Double-O's shoulder. They quickly run out of the snow cave. The bear is chasing them. It is still growling and looks angry.

The bear chases them all the way into town. Double-O and Phustus find their way to the ski lodge and hide inside.

When the bear goes away, they decide to go back and follow the trail of electric poles.

GO TO PAGE 46.

The Case of
the Mysterious
Menace in Venice

Double-O Phudd and Phustus arrive in Venice, Italy. The city of Venice is known for its canals, which are like streets filled with water. Most people use motorboats to get around. But tourists like the gondola, an old-fashioned boat. A pole is used to push it.

"What a wonderful old city this is!" Double-O says. Phustus is poling their gondola through the water. "There's no other place like it in the world!"

Double-O looks at the ornate buildings and bridges. Under a bridge nearby he notices a group of people wearing diving outfits.

"Look at that, Phusty," Double-O says. "A diving class under the bridge. How interesting."

Phustus squeaks as he poles.

"It is so peaceful in Venice," Double-O announces, ready to lie back in the gondola.

But Double-O sees something odd.

"Wait a minute," Double-O says. "Wasn't there a gondola right in front of us a second ago?"

Phutus looks confused.

"Help! Help! Someone sank my gondola!" someone cries. Double-O sees a man in the water.

"Quick, Phusty," Double-O says. "We must get over there and help!"

Phustus begins to pole as fast as he can.

"Oh, no!" Double-O cries. "Look over there! Another gondola is sinking! And another one over there!"

Double-O and Phustus arrive near where the first gondola sank. They pull the man out of the water.

"What happened?" Double-O asks.

GO TO PAGE 57.

"I don't know," the man answers. "I was just poling peacefully along. All of a sudden my gondola sank."

"Hmmm," says Double-O. "That is quite strange."

Phustus begins to squeak loudly. He points his paw down at the water.

"What is it, little fella?" Double-O asks. He looks at the water. "Oh, I see. Bubbles! Bubbles leading over toward the bridge! Should we follow those bubbles? Or should we first take a closer look at the sunken gondola? I wonder how it was sunk."

SHOULD DOUBLE-O INSPECT THE SUNKEN GONDOLA? TURN TO PAGE 58.

IF YOU THINK DOUBLE-O SHOULD FOLLOW THE BUBBLES, TURN TO PAGE 61.

"We'd better look at the bottom of that gondola. Let's see what made it sink," Double-O says as he dives into the water.

"There's a large round hole in the bottom," Double-O says to himself. "That's why it sank."

Double-O swims to his waiting gondola.

"Let's go to the bridge, Phusty," says Double-O. "I think we will find our boat-sinker there."

At the bridge Double-O asks the divers to walk by him, one at a time. Two divers are dripping wet—a man holding a saw and a woman holding a drill.

Double-O now knows whom he should accuse.

SHOULD DOUBLE-O ACCUSE THE MAN?
TURN TO PAGE 60.

IF YOU THINK DOUBLE-O SHOULD ACCUSE THE WOMAN,
TURN TO PAGE 64.

"We should head for the bridge. We can wait for that diver there," Double-O says to Phustus. "Step on it, Phusty!"

The gondola heads for the bridge. Another gondola sails right in front of them. They must stop.

"Hey! Watch where you're going!" Double-O yells. "We are trying to catch a criminal!"

"I'm terribly sorry," a man yells back. "I'm still learning to pole my gondola. I haven't quite got the hang of it yet."

Double-O helps to push the man's gondola out of their path.

They arrive at the bridge. There, Double-O announces to the divers that he wants them to line up. He needs to take a look at them. They form a line. Double-O notices that two of them are dripping wet.

"It must be one of those two," Double-O whispers to Phustus.

Double-O takes a closer look. One diver is a man, and the other is a woman. In a moment, Double-O knows whom he should accuse.

IF YOU THINK DOUBLE-O SHOULD ACCUSE THE MAN, TURN TO PAGE 63.

IF YOU THINK DOUBLE-O SHOULD ACCUSE THE WOMAN, TURN TO PAGE 64.

"All of you may go on with your diving class now," Double-O announces. "Except the man with the saw."

"You have been making big round holes in all the gondolas in Venice!" Double-O says.

"No, sir, actually I have not," the man answers. "You just said the holes in the gondolas were *round*. Look at my hand saw! I couldn't have sawed such perfect circles!"

"You have a point there," Double-O says. He looks down. Someone is drilling a hole in his gondola.

Double-O grabs a fishnet, throws it into the water, and catches a diver with a drill.

Double-O smiles. But the gondola—and Double-O and Phustus—sink slowly into the water.

THE END

"We better follow those bubbles. Quickly, before it's too late," Double-O says. "Pole rapidly, Phusty!"

Phustus goes to work.

"Those bubbles are heading for the bridge," Double-O says. "They are moving fast. The diver must be wearing flippers. And he probably has an air tank as well."

But then Double-O says, "Wait a minute, Phusty. The bubbles have stopped! I wonder what has happened."

Phustus stops the gondola.

"I'll bet that sneaky diver is hiding. But what should we do? We can't be sure. Should I dive into the water and try to catch the diver? Or should we pole to the bridge? We can wait for the diver there."

DO YOU THINK DOUBLE-O SHOULD ASK PHUSTUS TO POLE TO THE BRIDGE?
TURN TO PAGE 59.

SHOULD DOUBLE-O DIVE INTO THE WATER AND TRY TO CATCH THE DIVER?
TURN TO PAGE 62.

Without a thought, Double-O dives into the water. He swims to the bottom and looks in all directions.

A diver is swimming toward Phustus's gondola. The diver wears flippers, an air tank, and a mask.

Before Double-O can reach the gondola, the nasty diver tips it over. Phustus and the man from the sunken gondola tumble into the water.

The diver swims away quickly.

Double-O swims over to Phustus and the man. They are trying to stay afloat.

There's only one thing to do. They swim to shore and empty the water out of the gondola. Then they pole quickly toward the bridge.

GO TO PAGE 59.

Double-O points to the dripping man. "I noticed those flippers on your feet, sir," Double-O says. "And you are still dripping wet. That is how I knew it was you."

"I am a police officer, sir," the man answers. "I was working undercover. I must catch the mysterious gondola sinker. I almost had her, too! But now you have ruined my plans! Thanks to you, I may not find her!"

Double-O turns to Phustus and shrugs his shoulders.

"Chalk up another one to experience, little buddy," he says. "Let's get moving. I want to see Venice. Maybe we'll do better on our next case."

Phustus nods and hands Double-O the pole.

THE END

"Thank you all for lining up," Double-O says. "You may all go on with your class. Except for this woman over here.

"You cannot hide that drill from me," Double-O says. "I know you are sinking all the gondolas in Venice! What have you got to say for yourself?"

"Darn it all," the woman answers. "You got me."

"But why did you do it?" Double-O asks.

"My father owns a towel store. It's on that street over there," the woman says. "And his business has been bad lately. I just wanted to help him."

"Well, that is certainly no way to do it," says Double-O.

"Yes, I'm sorry," the woman answers. "I will never do it again."

"Do you promise?" asks Double-O.

"Yes, I do," says the woman.

Phustus pulls on Double-O's leg.

"You think we should let her go, don't you little buddy?" Double-O asks his friend.

Phustus squeaks a big yes.

"All right," says Double-O. "I'll let you go this time. But don't ever let it happen again."

"Oh, thank you," the woman says with a smile.

"It's all in a day's work for the greatest detective in the world, my dear," Double-O announces with a laugh. "All in a day's work."

THE END